Can you find
these bugs?

14 honeybees

1 tarantula

12 fire ants

7 Christmas
beetles

4 praying mantises

TWIG

For Saxon, whose curiosity and
love of insects inspired this book.

Scholastic Canada Ltd.
604 King Street West, Toronto, Ontario M5V 1E1, Canada

Scholastic Inc.
557 Broadway, New York, NY 10012, USA

Scholastic Australia Pty Limited
PO Box 579, Gosford, NSW 2250, Australia

Scholastic New Zealand Limited
Private Bag 94407, Botany, Manukau 2163, New Zealand

Scholastic Children's Books
Euston House, 24 Eversholt Street, London NW1 1DB, UK

www.scholastic.ca

The artwork in this book was created using watercolour,
coloured pencils and artline pens on watercolour paper,
with digital composition.

Library and Archives Canada Cataloguing in Publication

Parker, Aura, author, illustrator
    Twig / Aura Parker.

ISBN 978-1-4431-5793-3 (hardcover).--ISBN 978-1-4431-5794-0
(softcover)
I. Title.
PZ7.1.P37 Twi 2017   j823'.92   C2016-907993-7

First published by Scholastic Australia in 2016.
This edition published by Scholastic Canada in 2017.
Text and illustrations copyright © 2016 Aura Parker.

5 4 3 2 1   Printed in China   LFA   17 18 19 20 21

TWIG

Aura Parker

Scholastic Canada Ltd.
Toronto New York London Auckland Sydney
Mexico City New Delhi Hong Kong Buenos Aires

Bug School was abuzz with hundreds of shiny, scurrying shapes.

But not one bug noticed the new girl, Heidi,
tall and long like the twig of a tree.

Heidi waved hello to everyone.
But her teacher didn't even look up
from her looping and threading.

Scarlett and the spiderlings didn't see her.

Nor did the cockroach twins,

or the stinky bug,

or little Midge.

Miss Orb was a golden silk weaver
and a web-spinning champion.

"Good morning, class," she said,
as she hung up her weaving . . .

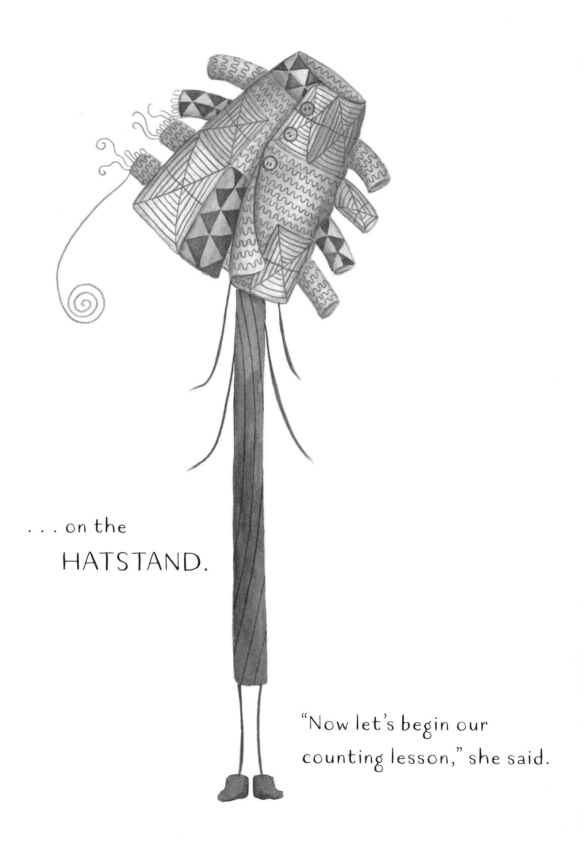

. . . on the
HATSTAND.

"Now let's begin our
counting lesson," she said.

One, two, three.

One, two, three.

I'm not a hatstand,

can't you see?

Heidi stood as still and straight as a twig.

The classroom was a flurry
of counting and colour.

But nobody noticed Heidi.

Nobody saw her
at lunchtime.

Nobody saw her here . . .

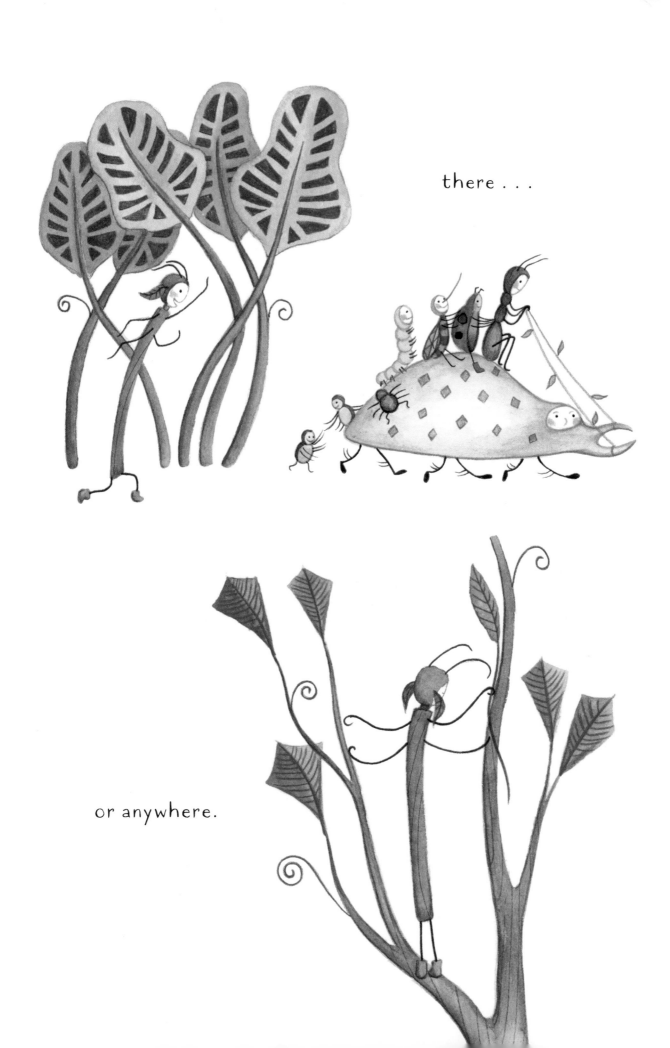

there . . .

or anywhere.

Nobody noticed Heidi at all.

One, two, three.

One, two, three.

'Why won't someone

play with me?

Miss Orb loved teaching everybody how to weave.
Weaving was tricky, with

sticky,

fiddly

threads.

Midge needed a little bit of help
from the cockroach twins.

The spiderlings did really well.

Stinky bug made a present for Nana.

And Scarlett found lots of
things to add to her weaving.

An interesting leaf,

a piece of bark shaped like a heart,

 a blue crackly pebble

 and a sprinkle of dirt.

Then she found a twig.

The twig let out a surprised yelp.

"I'm NOT a twig!
I'm me! I'm Heidi!"

And for the very first time, everyone saw her.
"Oops," said Scarlett. "You look so much like a twig!"
"Oh, there you are, Heidi!" said Miss Orb.
"It seems your camouflage has been working *too* well!"

Midge just stared, for he could
hardly believe it.

Miss Orb had a wonderful idea.

"Let's welcome Heidi to our class by weaving her a scarf. Everybody can make a square and we'll sew them together. Then, we'll be able to see her wherever she is!"

They looped and threaded and spun
all afternoon. Heidi joined in too.

It was the best weaving they
had ever done.

Heidi smiled and spun and twirled.
She loved her new scarf . . .

. . . and everyone could
see how happy she was.

These days, Heidi
always finds friends
in the playground.

She takes care of gaps when
they go on adventures.

Heidi helps reach things up high.

She even discovered a talent for basketball!

And Heidi always wears her scarf, except when it's time to play . . .

. . . her favourite game,

hide-and-seek.

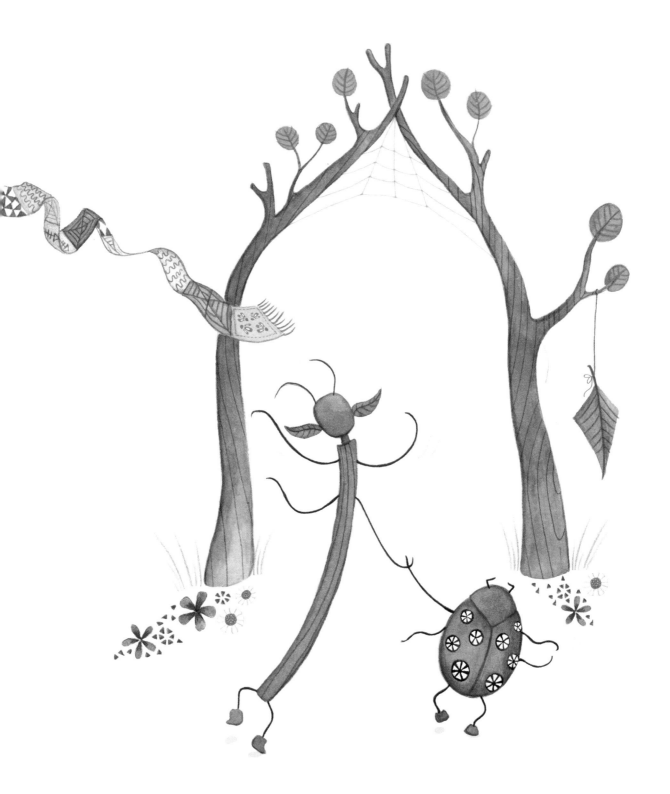

Can you find these bugs?

6 red-back spiders

2 cocoons

1 caterpillar

1 moth

18 leaf insects

. . . 10 9 8 7 6 5 4 3 2 1